To my friends who never do that, of course.
—Benjamin

Text copyright © 2019 by Davide Cali.
Illustrations copyright © 2019 by Benjamin Chaud.

Library of Congress Cataloging-in-Publication Data available.

ISBN 978-1-4521-3169-6

Manufactured in China.

Art direction by Naomi Kirsten.
Design by Ryan Hayes.
Cover design by Julia Marvel.
Typeset in ITC Century.
The illustrations in this book were rendered in pencil and digitally.

10 9 8 7 6 5 4 3 2 1

Chronicle Books LLC
680 Second Street
San Francisco, California 94107

Chronicle Books—we see things differently.
Become part of our community at www.chroniclekids.com.

Grown-ups Never Do That

Davide Cali

Benjamin Chaud

chronicle books · san francisco

Adults never misbehave.

They're never selfish.

They never yell.

They never interrupt.

They never cry.

They never say bad words.

They're never clumsy.

They never make funny faces.

They never lose their temper.

Adults are never wrong.

Ever.

They never cheat.

They never sulk.

They
never
forget.

They never
blame.

They're never messy.

And they're never ever late.

They never speak with their mouths full.

They never burp.

They never complain . . .
especially about waking up.

They never
neglect their
chores.

They never waste time.

They never litter.

Adults are always good.

So you really should be just like them.

Understand?

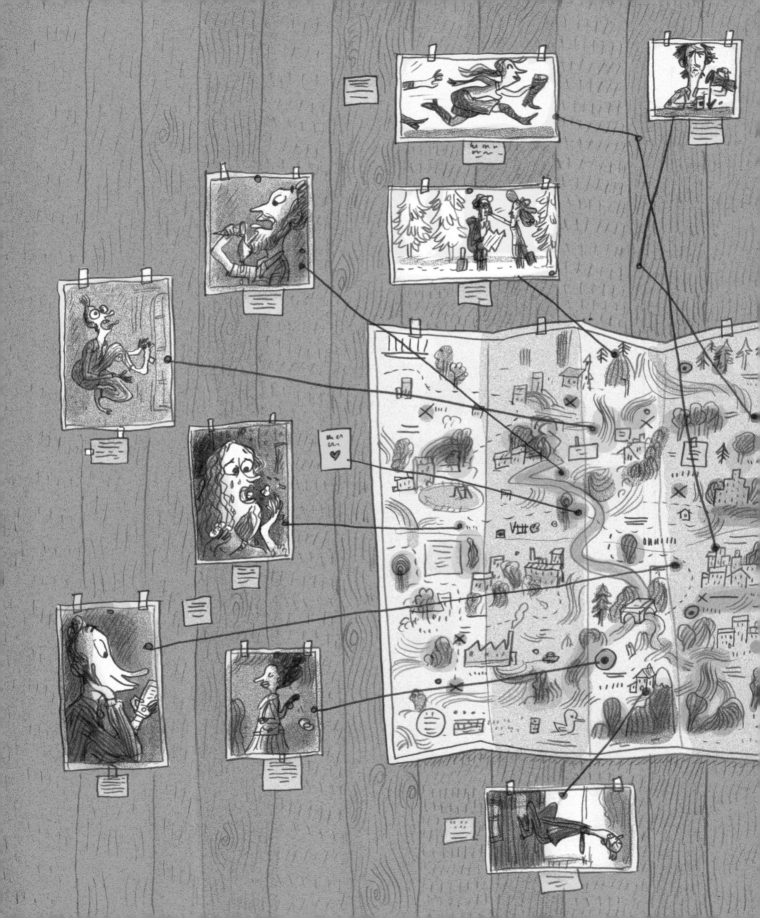